Clifford's
RIDDLES

by NORMAN BRIDWELL

SCHOLASTIC BOOK SERVICES

NEW YORK • TORONTO • LONDON • AUCKLAND • SYDNEY • TOKYO

To Christopher and Paul

Copyright © 1974 by Norman Bridwell. All rights reserved. Published by Scholastic Book Services, a division of Scholastic Magazines, Inc.

15 14 13 12 11 10 9 8 7 6 5   8 9/7 01/8

Printed in the U.S.A.

07

I'm Emily Elizabeth.
I want you to meet my dog, Clifford.

He's the biggest, reddest dog on the block.
He's smart too. He made up these riddles.

Why did Clifford sit on Emily Elizabeth's wrist and go "Tick-tock, tick-tock"?

He wanted to be a watchdog.

What is wet and pink
and holds fifty cans of dog food?

Clifford's tongue.

What is the difference between
a meeting of Sioux Indians
and Clifford's bark?

One is a big red pow-wow.
The other is a big red BOW-WOW.

What do you call a wet pup?

A soggy doggy.

What would be a good job for Clifford?

He could be a Seeing Eye dog for King Kong.

What would make a good belt for an elephant?

Clifford's collar.

If a German shepherd marries a Chihuahua, what will their child be?

A police dog that arrests midgets.

It's sweet. It's furry. It barks.
And it's frozen on a stick.
What is it?

A pup-sicle.

What floats on water,
is yellow,
goes "quack, quack,"
and weighs a hundred pounds?

Clifford's rubber ducky.

If your dog kisses you,
what do you call it?

A pooch smooch.

Where do you find bullies
that pick on Clifford's friends?

Far, far away.

If a dog marries a very small fish,
what will their baby be?

A guppy puppy.

What is black and white and red all over?

Clifford dressed up as a zebra.

What is made of leather,
has a loop at one end,
and runs around the block?

Clifford's leash.

What is the difference between
a hole in the road filled with water
and a sad French dog?

One is a muddy puddle. The other is a moody poodle.

Who carries a flashlight and looks very nervous?

A vet checking Clifford's tonsils.

If a bloodhound marries a bat,
what will their child be?

A vampire dog.

It's safe when it's sad.
But when it's happy – watch out!
What is it?

Clifford's tail.

What did Clifford do to get rid of dog pounds?

He went on a diet.

Name two kinds of wood you would use
if you made a statue of Clifford.

Giant redwood and dogwood.

He is faster than a speeding greyhound.
He is stronger than a Great Dane.
And he can leap over a dog catcher
in a single bound.
Who is he?

Super Pooch.

What is twelve feet tall,
stops at stop lights,
and has training wheels?

Clifford's bicycle.